Printed in the United States of America

Based on the Pooh Stories by A. A. Milne (copyright The Pooh Properties Trust).

First Edition

9 10

ISBN: 0-7868-3317-3

Visit www.disneybooks.com

CONTENTS

Tiggers Hate
to Lose

Isabel Gaines

ILLUSTRATED BY Francesc Rigol

One fine spring day,

while bouncing beside the stream,

Tigger found Pooh and his friends

standing on the bridge.

They were all staring into the water.

"What are you doing?" Tigger asked.

"We're playing Pooh Sticks," said Pooh.

"Tiggers love Pooh Sticks!" said Tigger.

"What's Pooh Sticks?"

"It's a game," said Pooh.

"Get some sticks,

and you can play, too."

Tigger found some sticks
and bounced back to the bridge.

"The first stick to pass
under the bridge wins,"
explained Rabbit.
"On your mark, get set . . . go!"

Pooh, Piglet, Rabbit,
Roo, and Eeyore
threw their sticks
into the water.

Tigger decided to watch once
before trying it himself.

Then they all raced
to the other side
of the bridge
to see who won.

"I can see mine!" Roo shouted.

"I win!"

But just as he said the words,

Roo's "stick" spread its wings

and flew up

to join the other dragonflies.

"Can you see yours, Pooh?" Piglet asked.

"No," Pooh replied.

"I expect my stick is stuck."

"Look," Rabbit cried.

"There's Eeyore's stick!"

"Oh, joy," muttered Eeyore.

"I won."

17

"Step aside," Tigger said.

"Tiggers are great at Pooh Sticks."

Everyone moved over
so Tigger could play, too.
Once again, Rabbit gave the signal,
"On your mark, get set . . . go!"

They tossed their sticks
off the bridge . . .

. . . then raced to the other side.

Tigger shouted, "Did I win?"

"Nope," mumbled Eeyore. "I did."

"Oh," said Tigger, frowning.

"Well, I was just warming up.

Let's play again."

They played again,
and just like before,
Eeyore's stick sailed past the others.

"Tiggers don't like losing,"
grumbled Tigger.
"Let's play again."

Eeyore won the next game, too.

"Oooh, goody," Eeyore said.

"I've won four times in a row."

Eeyore won the next time,

and the next time,

and the time after that, too.

"I just can't lose," muttered Eeyore.

Tigger stamped his foot.

"Let's play again," he said.

"Tiggers *hate* to lose."

During the next game,
at the very last moment,
Eeyore's stick
squeaked by Tigger's.

Tigger threw down his sticks.
"Tiggers don't like Pooh Sticks!"
he cried.

Tigger walked away
with his head down
and no bounce at all.

"I'll tell you my secret,"
Eeyore called.
"You have to drop your stick
in a twitchy sort of way."

Tigger bounced back
to the bridge.
This time when he
dropped his stick,
Tigger made sure to twitch.

And this time,

Tigger's stick won!

Tigger was so happy,

he began bouncing again.

And he bounced right into Eeyore.

The Giving Bear

Isabel Gaines

ILLUSTRATED BY Josie Yee

"Umph!" grunted Piglet
as he knocked on Pooh's door.
He had his wagon with him.
It was loaded with stuff.

"Hello, Piglet," answered Pooh.

"What's in your wagon?"

"Things from my house,"
Piglet said. "I'm giving them
to Christopher Robin."

Just then Tigger bounced up.

"Hello!" he said.

He had his wagon, too.

"Hello, Tigger," said Pooh.
"Are you giving your things
to Christopher Robin, too?"

"Yes," answered Tigger.
"So he can give them
to someone who needs them."

"Do you have anything
you don't need anymore,
Pooh?" asked Piglet.

"Let me think," said Pooh,
thinking very hard.
But he couldn't think
of a thing.

Along came Christopher Robin.

"I see Piglet's and Tigger's wagons,"
he said. "Are you going
to add anything, Pooh?"

"I don't have anything
to give away,"
Pooh said sadly.
"There must be something,"
said Tigger.

"Let's look in the cupboard,"

suggested Piglet.

Pooh opened the cupboard doors.

"Oh, dear!" said Piglet.

"Zowee!" shouted Tigger.

"Wow!" exclaimed Christopher Robin.

"Twenty honeypots!" they said
at the same time.

"Only ten honeypots

have any honey

in them," Christopher Robin said.

"I keep a large supply
of honeypots at all times,"
said Pooh.

"Why is that, Pooh Bear?"
asked Christopher Robin.
"Just in case," announced Pooh.

"In case of what?" asked Piglet.

He was a little afraid

to hear the answer.

"I might find
some especially
yummy honey," Pooh said.

"I would need plenty of pots
to store it in,
so I would never run out."

"ALL honey tastes
especially yummy to you!"
Christopher Robin
reminded Pooh gently.

"Ten pots are more than enough
to store your yummy honey."

"But what if I had a party?"
asked Pooh.
"Everyone would want
some honey,
so I would need a lot."

"Pooh," Christopher Robin said,
"if you had a party,
you would invite your friends
in the Hundred-Acre Wood."

"Ten honeypots hold
more than enough honey
for us," said Piglet.

"Hmm," said Pooh.
He still wasn't sure
he wanted to give away
his honeypots.

"Think of everyone
who could enjoy some honey
if you shared your honeypots,"
said Christopher Robin.

"Then they would all be
as happy as I am!" agreed Pooh.
Pooh decided to give away
ten of his honeypots.
His heart felt twice its size.

"Silly old bear," said Christopher Robin.
He helped Pooh load
his honeypots onto his wagon.

Eeyore Finds Friends

ADAPTED BY Isabel Gaines

ILLUSTRATED BY Josie Yee

One lovely spring morning,
Gopher popped out of a hole
right beside Eeyore.

"Say, sonny," said Gopher,
"why are you alone?
Don't you know
today is *Twos*-day?

"You should be with a friend.
One friend plus one friend
equals *Twos*-day."

"I see," said Eeyore sadly.

Then he perked up.

"Aren't you my friend, Gopher?"

"Of course I am," replied Gopher. "But I promised to spend the day with Rabbit. Good-bye, sonny, and good luck!"

Eeyore thought he would try
his luck with Owl,
so he set off into the woods.

Everywhere Eeyore looked,

he saw animals in pairs.

He saw two chipmunks . . .

and two possums . . .

and two bluebirds.

Eeyore hoped that Owl

was not part of a pair.

But as Eeyore walked

up to Owl's house,

he saw that Owl had a guest.

Owl and Kanga were having
a tea party outside with an iced cake
and everything.

"I get it," Eeyore muttered.

"Tea for two on *Twos*-day.

How nice."

As Eeyore walked away,

he saw two butterflies

fluttering above a flower.

There were two worms

inching along the path.

And two strange creatures
bouncing in the meadow.

Eeyore noticed that the creatures
were Tigger and Roo.

"I'm no good at bouncing, anyway,"
Eeyore told himself,
watching from behind a tree.

As Eeyore turned away,
he remembered that he had
only two more friends to see.

"Pooh and Piglet are probably spending *Twos*-day together," Eeyore mumbled. "But who knows? Maybe I'll get lucky."

But as Eeyore suspected,

Piglet was not at home.

Piglet was at Pooh's house.
Eeyore watched the pair
through the window.

"Oh, well," Eeyore sighed.
"I might as well go home
and sleep until *Winds*-day."

Just then Pooh saw Eeyore,

and hurried to the door.

"Hello, Eeyore," Pooh called.

"Would you like to join us for a snack?

We're having my favorite—honey."

"But that would ruin *Twos*-day," said Eeyore.

"Today is *Twos*-day?" asked Pooh.

"I forgot."

Pooh scratched his head and thought.
Finally he said, "*Twos*-day
could *stay* forgotten!

"We could call today *Fun*-day, instead.

It rhymes with Monday."

"I see," said Eeyore, though he didn't.

Eeyore followed Pooh inside
and the three friends had a *Fun*-day,
which was three times as nice
as a *Twos*-day!

Pooh's Surprise Basket

ADAPTED BY Isabel Gaines

ILLUSTRATED BY Josie Yee

The first of May
was a beautiful spring day.

Pooh decided to take a walk.

Pooh loved this time of year.

He sang a tune about it:

"Oh, I love spring.

Dum-dee dum-dum.

It makes me sing.

Pum-dee pum-pum.

"I pick spring flowers.
Dum-dee dum-dum.

I could do that for hours!
Pum-dee pum-pum."

At home, Pooh looked
at all the flowers
he had picked.

"These flowers are so pretty,"
he said.
"I should share them
with my friends."

Pooh got an idea.

"I can surprise everyone

with flower baskets

made just for them."

Pooh got right to work.

Pooh started with Piglet's basket.

He gathered clover and buttercups,

the smallest flowers he had picked.

He put them in the smallest basket.

Pooh held up Piglet's basket and smiled.
"A tiny basket," he said aloud.

"Tigger's turn!" said Pooh.

Pooh tossed a bunch

of flowers in the basket.

They went every which way.

"A messy basket," said Pooh.

For Rabbit, Pooh chose flowers
of the same color.
Carefully he cut them
all to the same size.

"A neat-and-tidy basket," he said.

For Roo's basket, Pooh
went to the cupboard.
He pulled out several bouncy balls.
He put them in the basket,
and added some flowers.

"A fun basket!" he said.

Pooh made a pretty basket for Kanga,

a wise basket for Owl,

and an Eeyore basket for Eeyore.

It was full of sticks and stones.

Pooh placed the last basket
on the table.

He was ready to make

Christopher Robin's basket.

He reached for the flowers.

But there was a problem.

NO MORE FLOWERS!

"Oh dear!" cried Pooh.
"What will I put
in Christopher Robin's basket?"

"Aha!" Pooh cried.
He tied a red ribbon
around the basket.

Then he gathered up
all the baskets
and ran out of the house.

Pooh left a basket at each
friend's house.

He went to Rabbit's house
and Piglet's house,
Tigger's, Eeyore's, and Owl's.

Then he stopped by
Kanga and Roo's.
He went to Christopher Robin's
house last.

Christopher Robin was outside.
"Christopher Robin," said Pooh,
"I surprised everyone
with flower baskets.

But I wanted to give you
something extra-special."
Pooh sat down inside the basket
and said, "This is a Pooh basket.
I made it just for you!"

"Silly old bear,"
said Christopher Robin.
"You are the best surprise ever!"

Be Quiet, Pooh!

Isabel Gaines

ILLUSTRATED BY Josie Yee

The sun streamed in
through Pooh's window.
"What a happy day!" he said.

Pooh got out of bed.

He stretched up.

He stretched down.

Then he ate
a big jar of honey.

It was nice outside,

so Pooh decided to take a walk.

While Pooh walked,
he made up a song.
"I had some honey.
Today is so sunny.
Hum, dee, ho, hummy."

Soon Pooh came
to Rabbit's house.
"Hum, dee, dee,
dum, dum," Pooh sang.

Rabbit poked his head
out of his window.
"Pooh, you woke
me up!" said Rabbit.

137

"I'm sorry," said Pooh.

"Would you like to sing with me?"

"No," said Rabbit.

Rabbit slammed his window shut
and went back to bed.
Pooh continued on his walk.

The next day was also
bright and sunny.
Pooh woke up
in a happy mood.

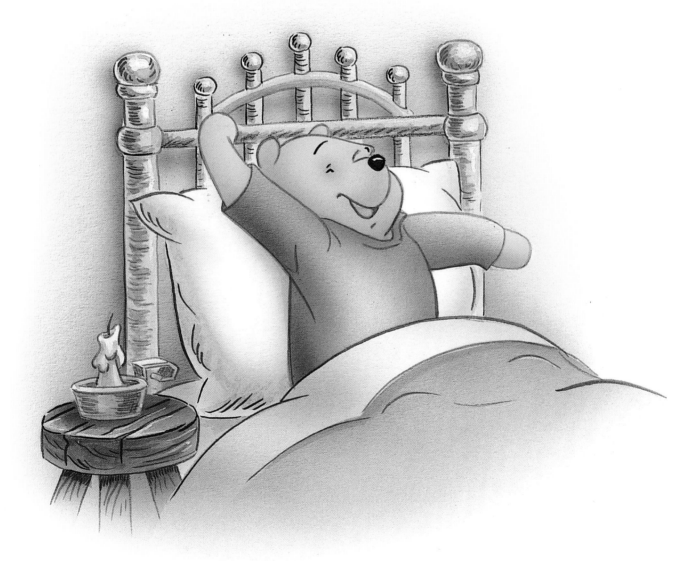

Pooh got out of bed.

He stretched up.

He stretched down.

Then he ate
a big jar of honey.

Once again,

he went out for a walk.

"The sun is so sunny,

I want more honey," sang Pooh.

When Pooh walked by Rabbit's house,
Pooh saw something new.

"Rabbit has a sign,
and it looks so fine,"
Pooh sang.

"Pooh, you woke me up again!"
shouted a sleepy Rabbit.
"Sorry, Rabbit," said Pooh.
"I like your new sign."

NO SINGING IN THE MORNING

"Thank you," said Rabbit.

"I made it. It says,

NO SINGING IN THE MORNING!"

"You did a very nice job,"

said Pooh.

The next morning,
Pooh decided to walk
in the other direction.

Rabbit slept happily
in his bed until he heard,
"Chirp, chirpety, chirp."
"Is that you, Pooh?" he called.

He looked out his window,
but Pooh was nowhere in sight.
Then Rabbit saw
a bird's nest on the sign.

149

"Chirp, chirpety, chirp,"
sang the baby birds
in the nest.
"Oh dear," said Rabbit.

He couldn't tell the baby birds
to be quiet.
They were so cute.
Their song was so sweet.

The next morning,
Rabbit awoke once again
to the baby birds singing.

He tried to be mad at them.

But as he listened to their song,

Rabbit discovered he rather liked it.

Then Rabbit heard Pooh
coming down the path.
Pooh was singing, too.
And his song matched
the baby birds' song.

Rabbit got an idea.

He jumped out of bed

and ran outside.

When Pooh arrived
at Rabbit's house,
he noticed Rabbit's sign
was different.

"What happened to your sign?"
asked Pooh.

"I fixed it," said Rabbit.

"Now it says,

PLEASE SING IN THE MORNING."

"What a wonderful idea!"

said Pooh.

"Would you like to join me
in a song or two now?"
"I most certainly would,"
said Rabbit.

And from that day on,
Pooh and Rabbit started every day
with a song.

Pooh's Scavenger Hunt

Isabel Gaines

ILLUSTRATED BY Studio Orlando

It was a sunny day in the Hundred-Acre Wood. Christopher Robin was sitting on a tree stump when Pooh and all his friends came to say hello.

"Hello, Christopher Robin," said Pooh.
"What are we going to do today?"

"Why don't we have
a scavenger hunt?"
said Christopher Robin.

"Tiggers love scavenger hunts!"
yelled Tigger.

"What is a scavenger hunt?"

"A scavenger hunt is a game
where you hunt for things,"
said Christopher Robin.

"What kinds of things?" asked Rabbit.
Christopher Robin scratched his head.
"Oh, let me think."

"Why don't you look for

a purple flower,

a small jar of honey,

and a red leaf?"

Christopher Robin smiled.
"And then,
I want you to find
the greatest thing
in the whole world."

Pooh was confused.
"Isn't honey the greatest thing
in the whole world?"
he asked.

"Honey is great,"
said Christopher Robin.
"But there is something
even greater."

So Pooh and his friends
went into the forest to search.

They went to Pooh's house first,
for that was the best place
to find honey.

"Up there is my only
small jar of honey,"
said Pooh.
"How will we
get it down?"

"Climb on my shoulders,"
said Tigger.

"I still can't reach it," said Pooh.

"Rabbit, can you help?"

"I can't quite reach.
Maybe if Roo helped, too?"
said Rabbit.

Roo grabbed the jar of honey,
and dropped it to Kanga.
Kanga put it in a bag.

"Next we need a leaf
and a flower," said Pooh.
"Does anybody remember
which should be red
and which should be purple?"
No one did.

"Well," said Pooh.

"Here is a red flower.

And it smells nice."

"Then it's perfect," said Kanga.

Everyone agreed.

"I found a leaf,"
Roo called.
"But it is not purple."

"I have some purple paint
at my house," said Rabbit.
"We can paint the leaf purple."
And that's what they did.

"Now all we need
is the greatest thing
in the whole world,"
said Piglet.

They headed back
into the woods.
"Greatest thing," called Pooh,
"where are you?"

They walked and walked.

Soon, it grew quite late—

and quite dark.

They all held hands

so no one would get lost.

Finally they found
Christopher Robin,
sitting on the tree stump.
They were back
where they had started.

"Hello," said
Christopher Robin.
"Are you done with
the scavenger hunt?"

"No," said Pooh sadly.

"We all searched together."

"And found everything," said Tigger.

"Except for the greatest thing
in the whole world,"
said Rabbit.

Christopher Robin smiled.
"But you did!
You found the greatest thing
in the whole world."

"We did?" they all asked.

"Oh, yes.

You searched together,"
said Christopher Robin.